AF347015

Robert Southey,
Charles Perrault,
The Brothers Grimm,
Aesop, Yei Theodora Ozaki,
Hans Christian Andersen,
Peter Christen Asbjørnsen,
Jørgen Moe,
Anonymous

GOLDILOCKS AND THE THREE BEARS

AND OTHER WRITINGS

DELHI OPEN BOOKS

**GOLDILOCKS AND THE THREE BEARS
AND OTHER WRITINGS**

by Robert Southey, Charles Perrault., The Brothers Grimm,
Aesop, Yei Theodora Ozaki, Hans Christian Andersen,
Peter Christen Asbjørnsen, Jørgen Moe, Anonymous

Edition copyright © Delhi Open Books, 2023

ALL RIGHTS RESERVED. No part of this publication may be reproduced, stored in a retrieval system, or transmitted, in any form or by any means, electronic, mechanical, photocopying, recording and or without permission of the publisher.

Published by

Delhi Open Books

G/F, 4771/23, Bharat Ram Road, Daryaganj, New Delhi-110002
Ph.: 91-11-42408081
E-mail: **delhiopenbooks2016@gmail.com**

ISBN: 978-81-961623-4-4

Cover, Typesetting, and Book Design by **ROHIT**

Contents

Goldilocks and The Three Bears

by Robert Southey

Once upon a time there were three Bears, who lived together in a house of their own, in a wood. One of them was a Little Wee Bear, and one was a Middle-sized Bear, and the other was a Great Big Bear. They had each a bowl for their porridge; a little bowl for the Little Wee Bear; and a middle-sized bowl for the Middle-sized Bear; and a great bowl for the Great Big Bear. And they had each a chair to sit in; a little chair for the Little Wee Bear; and a middle-sized chair for the Middle-sized Bear; and a great chair for the Great Big Bear. And they had each a bed to sleep in; a little bed for the Little Wee Bear; and a middle-sized bed for the Middle-sized Bear; and a great bed for the Great Big Bear.

One day, after they had made the porridge for their breakfast, and poured it into their porridge-bowls, they walked out into the wood while the porridge was cooling, that they might not burn their mouths by beginning too soon, for they were polite, well-brought-up Bears. And while they were away a little girl called Goldilocks, who lived at the other side of the wood and had been sent on an errand by her mother, passed by the house, and looked in at the window. And then she peeped in at the keyhole, for she was not at all a well-brought-up little girl. Then seeing nobody in the house she lifted the latch. The door was not fastened, because the Bears were good Bears, who did nobody any harm, and never suspected that anybody would harm them. So Goldilocks opened the door and went in; and well pleased was she when she saw the porridge on the table. If she had been a well-brought-up little girl she would have waited till the Bears came home, and then, perhaps, they would have asked her to breakfast; for they were good Bears—a little rough or so, as the manner of Bears is, but for all that very good-natured and hospitable. But she was an impudent, rude little girl, and so she set about helping herself.

First she tasted the porridge of the Great Big Bear, and that was too hot for her. Next she tasted the porridge of the Middle-sized Bear, but that was too cold for her. And then she went to the porridge of the Little Wee Bear, and tasted it, and that was neither too hot nor too cold, but just right, and she liked it so well that she ate it all up, every bit!

Then Goldilocks, who was tired, for she had been catching butterflies instead of running on her errand, sate down in the chair of the Great Big Bear, but that was too hard for her. And then she sate down in the chair of the Middle-sized Bear, and that was too soft for her. But when she sat down in the chair of the Little Wee Bear, that was neither too hard nor too soft, but just right. So she seated herself in it, and there she sate till the bottom of the chair came out, and down she came, plump upon the ground; and that made her very cross, for she was a bad-tempered little girl.

Now, being determined to rest, Goldilocks went upstairs into the bedchamber in which the Three Bears slept. And first she lay down upon the bed of the Great Big Bear, but that was too high at the head for her. And next she lay down upon the bed of the Middle-sized Bear, and that was too high at the foot for her. And then she lay down upon the bed of the Little Wee Bear, and that was neither too high at the head nor at the foot, but just right. So she covered herself up comfortably, and lay there till she fell fast asleep.

By this time the Three Bears thought their porridge would be cool enough for them to eat it properly; so they came home to breakfast. Now careless Goldilocks had left the spoon of the Great Big Bear standing in his porridge.

"SOMEBODY HAS BEEN AT MY PORRIDGE!"

said the Great Big Bear in his great, rough, gruff voice.

Then the Middle-sized Bear looked at his porridge and saw the spoon was standing in it too.

"SOMEBODY HAS BEEN AT MY PORRIDGE!"

said the Middle-sized Bear in his middle-sized voice.

Then the Little Wee Bear looked at his, and there was the spoon in the porridge-bowl, but the porridge was all gone!

"SOMEBODY HAS BEEN AT MY PORRIDGE, AND HAS EATEN IT ALL UP!"

said the Little Wee Bear in his little wee voice.

Upon this the Three Bears, seeing that some one had entered their house, and eaten up the Little Wee Bear's breakfast, began to look about them. Now the careless Goldilocks had not put the hard cushion straight when she rose from the chair of the Great Big Bear.

"SOMEBODY HAS BEEN SITTING IN MY CHAIR!"

said the Great Big Bear in his great, rough, gruff voice.

And the careless Goldilocks had squatted down the soft cushion of the Middle-sized Bear.

"SOMEBODY HAS BEEN SITTING IN MY CHAIR!"

said the Middle-sized Bear in his middle-sized voice.

"SOMEBODY HAS BEEN SITTING IN MY CHAIR, AND HAS SATE THE BOTTOM THROUGH!"

said the Little Wee Bear in his little wee voice.

Then the Three Bears thought they had better make

further search in case it was a burglar, so they went upstairs into their bedchamber. Now Goldilocks had pulled the pillow of the Great Big Bear out of its place.

"SOMEBODY HAS BEEN LYING IN MY BED!"

said the Great Big Bear in his great, rough, gruff voice.

And Goldilocks had pulled the bolster of the Middle-sized Bear out of its place.

"SOMEBODY HAS BEEN LYING IN MY BED!"

said the Middle-sized Bear in his middle-sized voice.

But when the Little Wee Bear came to look at his bed, there was the bolster in its place! And the pillow was in its place upon the bolster!

And upon the pillow——?

There was Goldilocks's yellow head—which was not in its place, for she had no business there.

"SOMEBODY HAS BEEN LYING IN MY BED,—AND HERE SHE IS STILL!"

said the Little Wee Bear in his little wee voice.

Now Goldilocks had heard in her sleep the great, rough, gruff voice of the Great Big Bear; but she was so fast asleep that it was no more to her than the roaring of wind, or the rumbling of thunder. And she had heard the middle-sized voice of the Middle-sized Bear, but it was only as if she had heard some one speaking in a dream. But when she heard the little wee voice of the Little Wee Bear, it was so sharp, and so shrill, that it awakened her at once. Up she started, and when she saw the Three Bears on one side of the bed, she tumbled herself out at the other, and ran to the window. Now the window was open, because the Bears, like good, tidy Bears, as they were, always opened their bedchamber window when they got up in the morning. So naughty, frightened little Goldilocks jumped; and whether she broke her neck in the fall, or ran into the wood and was lost there, or found her way out of the wood and got whipped for being a bad girl and playing truant, no one can say. But the Three Bears never saw anything more of her.

Cinderella

by Charles Perrault.

ONCE there was a gentleman who married, for his second wife, the proudest and most haughty woman that was ever seen. She had, by a former husband, two daughters of her own humor, who were, indeed, exactly like her in all things. He had likewise, by another wife, a young daughter, but of unparalleled goodness and sweetness of temper, which she took from her mother, who was the best creature in the world.

No sooner were the ceremonies of the wedding over but the mother-in-law began to show herself in her true colors. She could not bear the good qualities of this pretty girl, and the less because they made her own daughters appear the more odious. She employed her in the meanest work of the house: she scoured the dishes, tables, etc., and scrubbed madam's chamber, and those of misses, her daughters; she lay up in a sorry garret, upon a wretched straw bed, while her sisters lay in fine rooms, with floors all inlaid, upon beds of the very newest fashion, and where they had looking-glasses so large that they might see themselves at their full length from head to foot.

The poor girl bore all patiently, and dared not tell her father, who would have rattled her off; for his wife governed him entirely. When she had done her work, she used to go into the chimney-corner, and sit down among cinders and ashes, which made her commonly be called Cinderwench; but the youngest, who was not so rude and uncivil as the eldest, called her Cinderella. However, Cinderella, notwithstanding her mean apparel, was a hundred times handsomer than her sisters, though they were always dressed very richly.

It happened that the King's son gave a ball, and invited all persons of fashion to it. Our young misses were also invited, for they cut a very grand figure among the quality. They were mightily delighted at this invitation, and wonderfully busy in choosing out such gowns, petticoats, and head-clothes as might become them. This was a new trouble to Cinderella; for it was she who ironed her sisters' linen, and plaited their ruffles; they talked all day long of nothing but how they should be dressed.

"For my part," said the eldest, "I will wear my red velvet suit with French trimming."

"And I," said the youngest, "shall have my usual petticoat; but then, to make amends for that, I will put on my gold-flowered manteau, and my diamond stomacher, which is far from being the most ordinary one in the world."

They sent for the best tire-woman they could get to make up their head-dresses and adjust their double pinners, and they had their red brushes and patches from Mademoiselle de la Poche.

Cinderella was likewise called up to them to be consulted in all these matters, for she had excellent notions, and advised them always for the best, nay, and offered her services to dress their heads, which they were very willing she should do. As she was doing this, they said to her:

"Cinderella, would you not be glad to go to the ball?"

"Alas!" said she, "you only jeer me; it is not for such as I am to go thither."

"Thou art in the right of it," replied they; "it would make the people laugh to see a Cinderwench at a ball."

Anyone but Cinderella would have dressed their heads awry, but she was very good, and dressed them perfectly well They were almost two days without eating, so much were they transported with joy. They broke above a dozen laces in trying to be laced up close, that they might have a fine slender shape, and they were continually at their looking-glass. At last the happy day came; they went to Court, and Cinderella followed them with her eyes as long as she could, and when she had lost sight of them, she fell a-crying.

Her godmother, who saw her all in tears, asked her what was the matter.

"I wish I could--I wish I could--"; she was not able to speak the rest, being interrupted by her tears and sobbing.

This godmother of hers, who was a fairy, said to her, "Thou wishest thou couldst go to the ball; is it not so?"

"Y--es," cried Cinderella, with a great sigh.

"Well," said her godmother, "be but a good girl, and I will contrive that thou shalt go." Then she took her into her chamber, and said to her, "Run into the garden, and bring me a pumpkin."

Cinderella went immediately to gather the finest she could get, and brought it to her godmother, not being able to imagine how this pumpkin could make her go to the ball. Her godmother scooped out all the inside of it, having left nothing but the rind; which done, she struck it with her wand, and the pumpkin was instantly turned into a fine coach, gilded all over with gold.

She then went to look into her mouse-trap, where she found six mice, all alive, and ordered Cinderella to lift up a little the trapdoor, when, giving each mouse, as it went out, a little tap with her wand, the mouse was that moment turned into a fine horse, which altogether made a very fine set of six horses of a beautiful mouse-colored dapple-gray. Being at a loss for a coachman,

"I will go and see," says Cinderella, "if there is never a rat in the rat-trap--we may make a coachman of him."

"Thou art in the right," replied her godmother; "go and

look."

Cinderella brought the trap to her, and in it there were three huge rats. The fairy made choice of one of the three which had the largest beard, and, having touched him with her wand, he was turned into a fat, jolly coach- man, who had the smartest whiskers eyes ever beheld. After that, she said to her:

"Go again into the garden, and you will find six lizards behind the watering-pot, bring them to me."

She had no sooner done so but her godmother turned them into six footmen, who skipped up immediately behind the coach, with their liveries all bedaubed with gold and silver, and clung as close behind each other as if they had done nothing else their whole lives. The Fairy then said to Cinderella:

"Well, you see here an equipage fit to go to the ball with; are you not pleased with it?"

"Oh! yes," cried she; "but must I go thither as I am, in these nasty rags?"

Her godmother only just touched her with her wand, and, at the same instant, her clothes were turned into cloth of gold and silver, all beset with jewels. This done, she gave her a pair of glass slippers, the prettiest in the whole world. Being thus decked out, she got up into her coach; but her godmother, above all things, commanded her not to stay till after midnight, telling her, at the same time, that if she stayed one moment longer, the coach would be a pumpkin again, her horses mice, her coachman a rat, her footmen lizards, and her clothes become just as they were before.

She promised her godmother she would not fail of leaving the ball before midnight; and then away she drives, scarce able to contain herself for joy. The King's son who was told that a great princess, whom nobody knew, was come, ran out to receive her; he gave her his hand as she alighted out of the coach, and led her into the ball, among all the company. There was immediately a profound silence, they left off dancing, and the violins ceased to play, so attentive was everyone to contemplate the singular beauties of the unknown new-comer. Nothing was then heard but a confused noise of:

"Ha! how handsome she is! Ha! how handsome she is!"

The King himself, old as he was, could not help watching her, and telling the Queen softly that it was a long time since he had seen so beautiful and lovely a creature.

All the ladies were busied in considering her clothes and headdress, that they might have some made next day after the same pattern, provided they could meet with such fine material and as able hands to make them.

The King's son conducted her to the most honorable seat, and afterward took her out to dance with him; she danced so very gracefully that they all more and more admired her. A fine collation was served up, whereof the young prince ate not a morsel, so intently was he busied in gazing on her.

She went and sat down by her sisters, showing them a thousand civilities, giving them part of the oranges and citrons which the Prince had presented her with, which very much surprised them, for they did not know her. While Cinderella was thus amusing her sisters, she heard the clock strike eleven and three-quarters, whereupon she immediately made a courtesy to the company and hasted away as fast as she could.

When she got home she ran to seek out her godmother, and, after having thanked her, she said she could not but heartily wish she might go next day to the ball, because the King's son had desired her.

As she was eagerly telling her godmother whatever had passed at the ball, her two sisters knocked at the door, which Cinderella ran and opened.

"How long you have stayed!" cried she, gaping, rubbing her eyes and stretching herself as if she had been just waked out of her sleep; she had not, however, any manner of inclination to sleep since they went from home.

"If thou hadst been at the ball," said one of her sisters, "thou wouldst not have been tired with it. There came thither the finest princess, the most beautiful ever was seen with mortal eyes; she showed us a thousand civilities, and gave us oranges and citrons."

Cinderella seemed very indifferent in the matter; indeed, she asked them the name of that princess; but they told her they did not know it, and that the King's son was very uneasy on her account and would give all the world to know who she was. At this Cinderella, smiling, replied:

"She must, then, be very beautiful indeed; how happy you have been! Could not I see her? Ah! dear Miss Charlotte, do lend me your yellow suit of clothes which you wear every day."

"Ay, to be sure!" cried Miss Charlotte; "lend my clothes to such a dirty Cinderwench as thou art! I should be a fool."

Cinderella, indeed, expected well such answer, and was very glad of the refusal; for she would have been sadly put to it if her sister had lent her what she asked for jestingly.

The next day the two sisters were at the ball, and so was Cinderella, but dressed more magnificently than before. The King's son was always by her, and never ceased his compliments and kind speeches to her; to whom all this was so far from being tiresome that she quite forgot what her godmother had recommended to her; so that she, at last, counted the clock striking twelve when she took it to be no more than eleven; she then rose up and fled, as nimble as a deer. The Prince followed, but could not overtake her. She left behind one of her glass slippers, which the Prince took up most carefully. She got home but quite out of breath, and in her nasty old clothes, having nothing left her of all her finery but one of the little slippers, fellow to that she dropped. The guards at the palace gate were asked:

If they had not seen a princess go out.

Who said: They had seen nobody go out but a young girl, very meanly dressed, and who had more the air of a poor country wench than a gentlewoman.

When the two sisters returned from the ball Cinderella asked them: If they had been well diverted, and if the fine lady had been there.

They told her: Yes, but that she hurried away immediately when it struck twelve, and with so much haste that she dropped one of her little glass slippers, the prettiest in the world, which the King's son had taken up; that he had done nothing but look at her all the time at the ball, and that most certainly he was very much in love with the beautiful person who owned the glass slipper.

What they said was very true; for a few days after the King's son caused it to be proclaimed, by sound of trumpet, that he would marry her whose foot the slipper would just fit. They whom he employed began to try it upon the princesses, then the duchesses and all the Court, but in vain; it was brought to the two sisters, who did all they possibly could to thrust their foot into the slipper, but they could not effect it. Cinderella, who saw all this, and knew her slipper, said to them, laughing:

"Let me see if it will not fit me."

Her sisters burst out a-laughing, and began to banter her. The gentleman who was sent to try the slipper looked earnestly at Cinderella, and, finding her very handsome, said:

It was but just that she should try, and that he had orders to let everyone make trial.

He obliged Cinderella to sit down, and, putting the slipper

to her foot, he found it went on very easily, and fitted her as if it had been made of wax. The astonishment her two sisters were in was excessively great, but still abundantly greater when Cinderella pulled out of her pocket the other slipper, and put it on her foot. Thereupon, in came her godmother, who, having touched with her wand Cinderella's clothes, made them richer and more magnificent than any of those she had before.

And now her two sisters found her to be that fine, beautiful lady whom they had seen at the ball. They threw themselves at her feet to beg pardon for all the ill- treatment they had made her undergo. Cinderella took them up, and, as she embraced them, cried:

That she forgave them with all her heart, and desired them always to love her.

She was conducted to the young prince, dressed as she was; he thought her more charming than ever, and, a few days after, married her. Cinderella, who was no less good than beautiful, gave her two sisters lodgings in the palace.

The Elves and The Shoemaker

by The Brothers Grimm

FIRST STORY

A shoemaker, by no fault of his own, had become so poor that at last he had nothing left but leather for one pair of shoes. So in the evening, he cut out the shoes which he wished to begin to make the next morning, and as he had a good conscience, he lay down quietly in his bed, commended himself to God, and fell asleep. In the morning, after he had said his prayers, and was just going to sit down to work, the two shoes stood quite finished on his table. He was astounded, and knew not what to say to it. He took the shoes in his hands to observe them closer, and they were so neatly made that there was not one bad stitch in them, just as if they were intended as a masterpiece. Soon after, a buyer came in, and as the shoes pleased him so well, he paid more for them than was customary, and, with the money, the shoemaker was able to purchase leather for two pairs of shoes. He cut them out at night, and next morning was about to set to work with fresh courage; but he had no need to do so, for, when he got up, they were already made, and buyers also were not wanting, who gave him money enough to buy leather for four pairs of shoes. The following morning, too, he found the four pairs made; and so it went on constantly, what he cut out in the evening was finished by the morning, so that he soon had his honest independence again, and at last became a wealthy man. Now it befell that one evening not long before Christmas, when the man had been cutting out, he said to his wife, before going to bed, "What think you if we were to stay up to-night to see who it is that lends us this helping hand?" The woman liked the idea, and lighted a candle, and then they hid themselves in a corner of the room, behind some clothes which were hanging up there, and watched. When it was midnight, two pretty little naked men came, sat down by the shoemaker's table, took all the work which was cut out before them and began to stitch, and sew, and hammer so skilfully and so quickly with their little fingers that the shoemaker could not turn away his eyes for astonishment. They did not stop until all was done, and stood finished on the table, and they ran quickly away.

Next morning the woman said, "The little men have made us rich, and we really must show that we are grateful for it. They run about so, and have nothing on, and must be cold. I'll tell thee what I'll do: I will make them little shirts, and coats, and vests, and trousers, and knit both of them a pair of stockings, and do thou, too, make them two little pairs of shoes." The man said, "I shall be very glad to do it;" and one night, when everything was ready, they laid their presents all together on the table instead of the cut-out work, and then concealed themselves to see how the little men would behave. At midnight they came bounding in, and wanted to get to work at once, but as they did not find any leather cut out, but only the pretty little articles of clothing, they were at first astonished, and then they showed intense delight. They dressed themselves with the greatest rapidity, putting the pretty clothes on, and singing,

"Now we are boys so fine to see,

Why should we longer cobblers be?"

Then they danced and skipped and leapt over chairs and benches. At last they danced out of doors. From that time forth they came no more, but as long as the shoemaker lived all went well with him, and all his undertakings prospered.

SECOND STORY

There was once a poor servant-girl, who was industrious and cleanly, and swept the house every day, and emptied her sweepings on the great heap in front of the door. One morning when she was just going back to her work, she found a letter on this heap, and as she could not read, she put her broom in the corner, and took the letter to her master and mistress, and behold it was an invitation from the elves, who asked the girl to hold a child for them at its christening. The girl did not know what to do, but at length, after much persuasion, and as they told her that it was not right to refuse an invitation of this kind, she consented. Then three elves came and conducted her to a hollow mountain, where the little folks lived. Everything there was small, but more elegant and beautiful than can be described. The baby's mother lay in a bed of black ebony ornamented with pearls, the coverlids were embroidered with gold, the cradle was of ivory, the bath of gold. The girl stood as godmother, and then wanted to go home again, but the little elves urgently entreated her to stay three days with them. So she stayed, and passed the time in pleasure and gaiety, and the little folks did all they could to make her happy. At last she set out on her way home. Then first they filled her pockets quite full of money, and after that they led her out of the mountain again. When she got home, she wanted to begin her work, and took the broom, which was still standing in the corner, in her hand and began to sweep. Then some strangers came out of the house, who asked her who she was, and what business she had there? And she had not, as she thought, been three days with the little men in the mountains, but seven years, and in the meantime her former masters had died.

THIRD STORY

A certain mother's child had been taken away out of its cradle by the elves, and a changeling with a large head and staring eyes, which would do nothing but eat and drink, laid in its place. In her trouble she went to her neighbour, and asked her advice. The neighbour said that she was to carry the changeling into the kitchen, set it down on the hearth, light a fire, and boil some water in two egg-shells, which would make the changeling laugh, and if he laughed, all would be over with him. The woman did everything that her neighbour bade her. When she put the egg-shells with water on the fire, the imp said, "I am as old now as the Wester Forest, but never yet have I seen any one boil anything in an egg-shell!" And he began to laugh at it. Whilst he was laughing, suddenly came a host of little elves, who brought the right child, set it down on the hearth, and took the changeling away with them.

The Lion And The Mouse

by Aesop

A Lion lay asleep in the forest, his great head resting on his paws. A timid little Mouse came upon him unexpectedly, and in her fright and haste to get away, ran across the Lion's nose. Roused from his nap, the Lion laid his huge paw angrily on the tiny creature to kill her.

"Spare me!" begged the poor Mouse. "Please let me go and some day I will surely repay you."

The Lion was much amused to think that a Mouse could ever help him. But he was generous and finally let the Mouse go.

Some days later, while stalking his prey in the forest, the Lion was caught in the toils of a hunter's net. Unable to free himself, he filled the forest with his angry roaring. The Mouse knew the voice and quickly found the Lion struggling in the net. Running to one of the great ropes that bound him, she gnawed it until it parted, and soon the Lion was free.

"You laughed when I said I would repay you," said the Mouse. "Now you see that even a Mouse can help a Lion."

A kindness is never wasted.

The Sagacious Monkey and the Boar

by Yei Theodora Ozaki

Long, long ago, there lived in the province of Shinshin in Japan, a traveling monkey-man, who earned his living by taking round a monkey and showing off the animal's tricks.

One evening the man came home in a very bad temper and told his wife to send for the butcher the next morning.

The wife was very bewildered and asked her husband:

"Why do you wish me to send for the butcher?"

"It's no use taking that monkey round any longer, he's too old and forgets his tricks. I beat him with my stick all I know how, but he won't dance properly. I must now sell him to the butcher and make what money out of him I can. There is nothing else to be done."

The woman felt very sorry for the poor little animal, and pleaded for her husband to spare the monkey, but her pleading was all in vain, the man was determined to sell him to the butcher.

Now the monkey was in the next room and overheard every word of the conversation. He soon understood that he was to be killed, and he said to himself:

"Barbarous, indeed, is my master! Here I have served him faithfully for years, and instead of allowing me to end my days comfortably and in peace, he is going to let me be cut up by the butcher, and my poor body is to be roasted and stewed and eaten? Woe is me! What am I to do. Ah! a bright thought has struck me! There is, I know, a wild bear living in the forest near by. I have often heard tell of his wisdom. Perhaps if I go to him and tell him the strait I am in he will give me his counsel. I will go and try."

There was no time to lose. The monkey slipped out of the house and ran as quickly as he could to the forest to find the boar. The boar was at home, and the monkey began his tale of woe at once.

"Good Mr. Boar, I have heard of your excellent wisdom. I am in great trouble, you alone can help me. I have grown old in the service of my master, and because I cannot dance properly now he intends to sell me to the butcher. What do you advise me to do? I know how clever you are!"

The boar was pleased at the flattery and determined to help the monkey. He thought for a little while and then said:

"Hasn't your master a baby?"

"Oh, yes," said the monkey, "he has one infant son."

"Doesn't it lie by the door in the morning when your mistress begins the work of the day? Well, I will come round early and when I see my opportunity I will seize the child and run off with it."

"What then?" said the monkey.

"Why the mother will be in a tremendous scare, and before your master and mistress know what to do, you must run after me and rescue the child and take it home safely to its parents, and you will see that when the butcher comes they won't have the heart to sell you."

The monkey thanked the boar many times and then went home. He did not sleep much that night, as you may imagine, for thinking of the morrow. His life depended on whether the boar's plan succeeded or not. He was the first up, waiting anxiously for what was to happen. It seemed to him a very long time before his master's wife began to move about and open the shutters to let in the light of day. Then all happened as the boar had planned. The mother placed her child near the porch as usual while she tidied up the house and got her breakfast ready.

The child was crooning happily in the morning sunlight, dabbing on the mats at the play of light and shadow. Suddenly there was a noise in the porch and a loud cry from the child. The mother ran out from the kitchen to the spot, only just in time to see the boar disappearing through the gate with her child in its clutch. She flung out her hands with a loud cry of despair and rushed into the inner room where her husband was still sleeping soundly.

He sat up slowly and rubbed his eyes, and crossly demanded what his wife was making all that noise about. By the time that the man was alive to what had happened, and they both got outside the gate, the boar had got well away, but they saw the monkey running after the thief as hard as his legs would carry him.

Both the man and wife were moved to admiration at the plucky conduct of the sagacious monkey, and their gratitude knew no bounds when the faithful monkey brought the child safely back to their arms.

"There!" said the wife. "This is the animal you want to kill—if the monkey hadn't been here we should have lost our child forever."

"You are right, wife, for once," said the man as he carried the child into the house. "You may send the butcher back when he comes, and now give us all a good breakfast and the monkey too."

When the butcher arrived he was sent away with an order for some boar's meat for the evening dinner, and the monkey was petted and lived the rest of his days in peace, nor did his master ever strike him again.

The Little Mermaid

by Hans Christian Andersen

Hans Christian Andersen's The Little Mermaid or 'Den lille Havfrue' (1837)

Far out in the ocean the water is as blue as the petals of the loveliest cornflower, and as clear as the purest glass. But it is very deep too. It goes down deeper than any anchor rope will go, and many, many steeples would have to be stacked one on top of another to reach from the bottom to the surface of the sea. It is down there that the sea folk live.

Now don't suppose that there are only bare white sands at the bottom of the sea. No indeed! The most marvelous trees and flowers grow down there, with such pliant stalks and leaves that the least stir in the water makes them move about as though they were alive. All sorts of fish, large and small, dart among the branches, just as birds flit through the trees up here. From the deepest spot in the ocean rises the palace of the sea king. Its walls are made of coral and its high pointed windows of the clearest amber, but the roof is made of mussel shells that open and shut with the tide. This is a wonderful sight to see, for every shell holds glistening pearls, any one of which would be the pride of a queen's crown.

The sea king down there had been a widower for years, and his old mother kept house for him. She was a clever woman, but very proud of her noble birth. Therefore she flaunted twelve oysters on her tail while the other ladies of the court were only allowed to wear six. Except for this she was an altogether praiseworthy person, particularly so because she was extremely fond of her granddaughters, the little sea princesses. They were six lovely girls, but the youngest was the most beautiful of them all. Her skin was as soft and tender as a rose petal, and her eyes were as blue as the deep sea, but like all the others she had no feet. Her body ended in a fish tail.

The whole day long they used to play in the palace, down in the great halls where live flowers grew on the walls. Whenever the high amber windows were thrown open the fish would swim in, just as swallows dart into our rooms when we open the windows. But these fish, now, would swim right up to the little princesses to eat out of their hands and let themselves be petted.

Outside the palace was a big garden, with flaming red and deep-blue trees. Their fruit glittered like gold, and their blossoms flamed like fire on their constantly waving stalks. The soil was very fine sand indeed, but as blue as burning brimstone. A strange blue veil lay over everything down there. You would have thought yourself aloft in the air with only the blue sky above and beneath you, rather than down at the bottom of the sea. When there was a dead calm, you could just see the sun, like a scarlet flower with light streaming from its calyx.

Each little princess had her own small garden plot, where she could dig and plant whatever she liked. One of them made her little flower bed in the shape of a whale, another thought it neater to shape hers like a little mermaid, but the youngest of them made hers as round as the sun, and there she grew only flowers which were as red as the sun itself. She was an unusual child, quiet and wistful, and when her sisters decorated their gardens with all kinds of odd things they had found in sunken ships, she would allow nothing in hers except flowers as red as the sun, and a pretty marble statue. This figure of a handsome boy, carved in pure white marble, had sunk down to the bottom of the sea from some ship that was wrecked. Beside the statue she planted a rose-colored weeping willow tree, which thrived so well that its graceful branches shaded the statue and hung down to the blue sand, where their shadows took on a violet tint, and swayed as the branches swayed. It looked as if the roots and the tips of the branches were kissing each other in play.

Nothing gave the youngest princess such pleasure as to hear about the world of human beings up above them. Her old grandmother had to tell her all she knew about ships and cities, and of people and animals. What seemed nicest of all to her was that up on land the flowers were fragrant, for those at the bottom of the sea had no scent. And she thought it was nice that the woods were green, and that the fish you saw among their branches could sing so loud and sweet that it was delightful to hear them. Her grandmother had to call the little birds "fish," or the princess would not have known what she was talking about, for she had never seen a bird.

"When you get to be fifteen," her grandmother said, "you will be allowed to rise up out of the ocean and sit on the rocks in the moonlight, to watch the great ships sailing by. You will see woods and towns, too."

Next year one of her sisters would be fifteen, but the others - well, since each was a whole year older than the next the youngest still had five long years to wait until she could rise up from the water and see what our world was like. But each sister promised to tell the others about all that she saw, and what she found most marvelous on her first day. Their grandmother had not told them half enough, and there were so many thing that they longed to know about.

The most eager of them all was the youngest, the very one who was so quiet and wistful. Many a night she stood by her open window and looked up through the dark blue water where the fish waved their fins and tails. She could just see the moon and stars. To be sure, their light was quite dim, but looked at through the water they seemed much bigger than they appear to us. Whenever a cloud-like shadow swept across them, she knew that it was either a whale swimming overhead, or a ship with many human beings aboard it. Little did they dream that a pretty young mermaid was down below, stretching her white arms up toward the keel of their ship.

The eldest princess had her fifteenth birthday, so now she received permission to rise up out of the water. When she got back she had a hundred things to tell her sisters about, but the most marvelous thing of all, she said, was to lie on a sand bar in the moonlight, when the sea was calm, and to gaze at the large city on the shore, where the lights twinkled like hundreds of stars; to listen to music; to hear the chatter and clamor of carriages and people; to see so many church towers and spires; and to hear the ringing bells. Because she could not enter the city, that was just what she most dearly longed to do.

Oh, how intently the youngest sister listened. After this, whenever she stood at her open window at night and looked up through the dark blue waters, she thought of that great city with all of its clatter and clamor, and even fancied that in these depths she could hear the church bells ring.

The next year, her second sister had permission to rise up to the surface and swim wherever she pleased. She came up just at sunset, and she said that this spectacle was the most marvelous sight she had ever seen. The heavens had a golden glow, and as for the clouds - she could not find words to describe their beauty. Splashed with red and tinted with violet, they sailed over her head. But much faster than the sailing clouds were wild swans in a flock. Like a long white veil trailing above the sea, they flew toward the setting sun. She too swam toward it, but down it went, and all the rose-colored glow faded from the sea and sky.

The following year, her third sister ascended, and as she was the boldest of them all she swam up a broad river that flowed into the ocean. She saw gloriously green, vine-colored hills. Palaces and manor houses could be glimpsed through the splendid woods. She heard all the birds sing, and the sun shone so brightly that often she had to dive under the water to cool her burning face. In a small cove she found a whole school of mortal children, paddling about in the water quite naked. She wanted to play with them, but they took fright and ran away. Then along came a little black animal - it was a dog, but she had never seen a dog before. It barked at her so ferociously that she took fright herself, and fled to the open sea. But never could she forget the splendid woods, the green hills, and the nice children who could swim in the water although they didn't wear fish tails.

The fourth sister was not so venturesome. She stayed far out among the rough waves, which she said was a marvelous place. You could see all around you for miles and miles, and the heavens up above you were like a vast dome of glass. She had seen ships, but they were so far away that they looked like sea gulls. Playful dolphins had turned somersaults, and monstrous whales had spouted water through their nostrils so that it looked as if hundreds of fountains were playing all around them.

Now the fifth sister had her turn. Her birthday came in the wintertime, so she saw things that none of the others had seen. The sea was a deep green color, and enormous icebergs drifted about. Each one glistened like a pearl, she said, but they were more lofty than any church steeple built by man. They assumed the most fantastic shapes, and sparkled like diamonds. She had seated herself on the largest one, and all the ships that came sailing by sped away as soon as the frightened sailors saw her there with her long hair blowing in the wind.

In the late evening clouds filled the sky. Thunder cracked and lightning darted across the heavens. Black waves lifted those great bergs of ice on high, where they flashed when the lightning struck.

On all the ships the sails were reefed and there was fear and trembling. But quietly she sat there, upon her drifting iceberg, and watched the blue forked lightning strike the sea.

Each of the sisters took delight in the lovely new sights when she first rose up to the surface of the sea. But when they became grown-up girls, who were allowed to go wherever they liked, they became indifferent to it. They would become homesick, and in a month they said that there was no place like the bottom of the sea, where they felt so completely at home.

On many an evening the older sisters would rise to the surface, arm in arm, all five in a row. They had beautiful voices, more charming than those of any mortal beings. When a storm was brewing, and they anticipated a shipwreck, they would swim before the ship and sing most seductively of how beautiful it was at the bottom of the ocean, trying to overcome the prejudice that the sailors had against coming down to them. But people could not understand their song, and mistook it for the voice of the storm. Nor was it for them to see the glories of the deep. When their ship went down they were drowned, and it was as dead men that they reached the sea king's palace.

On the evenings when the mermaids rose through the water like this, arm in arm, their youngest sister stayed behind all alone, looking after them and wanting to weep. But a mermaid has no tears, and therefore she suffers so much more.

"Oh, how I do wish I were fifteen!" she said. "I know I shall love that world up there and all the people who live in it."

And at last she too came to be fifteen.

"Now I'll have you off my hands," said her grandmother, the old queen dowager. "Come, let me adorn you like your sisters." In the little maid's hair she put a wreath of white lilies, each petal of which was formed from half of a pearl. And the old queen let eight big oysters fasten themselves to the princess's tail, as a sign of her high rank.

"But that hurts!" said the little mermaid.

"You must put up with a good deal to keep up appearances," her grandmother told her.

Oh, how gladly she would have shaken off all these decorations, and laid aside the cumbersome wreath! The red flowers in her garden were much more becoming to her, but she didn't dare to make any changes. "Good-by," she said, and up she went through the water, as light and as sparkling as a bubble.

The sun had just gone down when her head rose above the surface, but the clouds still shone like gold and roses, and in the delicately tinted sky sparkled the clear gleam of the evening star. The air was mild and fresh and the sea unruffled. A great three-master lay in view with only one of all its sails set, for there was not even the whisper of a breeze, and the sailors idled about in the rigging and on the yards. There was music and singing on the ship, and as night came on they lighted hundreds of such brightly colored lanterns that one might have thought the flags of all nations were swinging in the air.

The little mermaid swam right up to the window of the main cabin, and each time she rose with the swell she could peep in through the clear glass panes at the crowd of brilliantly dressed people within. The handsomest of them all was a young Prince with big dark eyes. He could not be more than sixteen years old. It was his birthday and that was the reason for all the celebration. Up on deck the sailors were dancing, and when the Prince appeared among them a hundred or more rockets flew through the air, making it as bright as day. These startled the little mermaid so badly that she ducked under the water. But she soon peeped up again, and then it seemed as if all the stars in the sky were falling around her. Never had she seen such fireworks. Great suns spun around, splendid fire-fish floated through the blue air, and all these things were mirrored in the crystal clear sea. It was so brilliantly bright that you could see every little rope of the ship, and the people could be seen distinctly. Oh, how handsome the young Prince was! He laughed, and he smiled and shook people by the hand, while the music rang out in the perfect evening.

It got very late, but the little mermaid could not take her eyes off the ship and the handsome Prince. The brightly colored lanterns were put out, no more rockets flew through the air, and no more cannon boomed. But there was a mutter and rumble deep down in the sea, and the swell kept bouncing her up so high that she could look into the cabin.

Now the ship began to sail. Canvas after canvas was spread in the wind, the waves rose high, great clouds gathered, and lightning flashed in the distance. Ah, they were in for a terrible storm, and the mariners made haste to reef the sails. The tall ship pitched and rolled as it sped through the angry sea. The waves rose up like towering black mountains, as if they would break over the masthead, but the swan-like ship plunged into the valleys between such waves, and emerged to ride their lofty heights. To the little mermaid this seemed good sport, but to the sailors it was nothing of the sort. The ship creaked and labored, thick timbers gave way under the heavy blows, waves broke over the ship, the mainmast snapped in two like a reed, the ship listed over on its side, and water burst into the hold.

Now the little mermaid saw that people were in peril, and that she herself must take care to avoid the beams and wreckage tossed about by the sea. One moment it would be black as pitch, and she couldn't see a thing. Next moment the lightning would flash so brightly that she could distinguish every soul on board. Everyone was looking out for himself as best he could. She watched closely for the young Prince, and when the ship split in two she saw him sink down in the sea. At first she was overjoyed that he would be with her, but then she recalled that human people could not live under the water, and he could only visit her father's palace as a dead man.

No, he should not die! So she swam in among all the floating planks and beams, completely forgetting that they might crush her. She dived through the waves and rode their crests, until at length she reached the young Prince, who was no longer able to swim in that raging sea. His arms and legs were exhausted, his beautiful eyes were closing, and he would have died if the little mermaid had not come to help him. She held his head above water, and let the waves take them wherever the waves went.

At daybreak, when the storm was over, not a trace of the ship was in view. The sun rose out of the waters, red and bright, and its beams seemed to bring the glow of life back to the cheeks of the Prince, but his eyes remained closed. The mermaid kissed his high and shapely forehead. As she stroked his wet hair in place, it seemed to her that he looked like that marble statue in her little garden. She kissed him again and hoped that he would live.

She saw dry land rise before her in high blue mountains, topped with snow as glistening white as if a flock of swans were resting there. Down by the shore were splendid green woods, and in the foreground stood a church, or perhaps a convent; she didn't know which, but anyway it was a building. Orange and lemon trees grew in its garden, and tall palm trees grew beside the gateway. Here the sea formed a little harbor, quite calm and very deep. Fine white sand had been washed up below the cliffs. She swam there with the handsome Prince, and stretched him out on the sand, taking special care to pillow his head up high in the warm sunlight.

The bells began to ring in the great white building, and a number of young girls came out into the garden. The little mermaid swam away behind some tall rocks that stuck out of the water. She covered her hair and her shoulders with foam so that no one could see her tiny face, and then she watched to see who would find the poor Prince.

In a little while one of the young girls came upon him. She seemed frightened, but only for a minute; then she called more people. The mermaid watched the Prince regain consciousness, and smile at everyone around him. But he did not smile at her, for he did not even know that she had saved him. She felt very unhappy, and when they led him away to the big building she dived sadly down into the water and returned to her father's palace.

She had always been quiet and wistful, and now she became much more so. Her sisters asked her what she had seen on her first visit up to the surface, but she would not tell them a thing.

Many evenings and many mornings she revisited the spot where she had left the Prince. She saw the fruit in the garden ripened and harvested, and she saw the snow on the high mountain melted away, but she did not see the Prince, so each time she came home sadder than she had left. It was her one consolation to sit in her little garden and throw her arms about the beautiful marble statue that looked so much like the Prince. But she took no care of her flowers now. They overgrew the paths until the place was a wilderness, and their long stalks and leaves became so entangled in the branches of the tree that it cast a gloomy shade.

Finally she couldn't bear it any longer. She told her secret to one of her sisters. Immediately all the other sisters heard about it. No one else knew, except a few more mermaids who told no one - except their most intimate friends. One of these friends knew who the Prince was. She too had seen the birthday celebration on the ship. She knew where he came from and where his kingdom was.

"Come, little sister!" said the other princesses. Arm in arm, they rose from the water in a long row, right in front of where they knew the Prince's palace stood. It was built of pale, glistening, golden stone with great marble staircases, one of which led down to the sea. Magnificent gilt domes rose above the roof, and between the pillars all around the building were marble statues that looked most lifelike. Through the clear glass of the lofty windows one could see into the splendid halls, with their costly silk hangings and tapestries, and walls covered with paintings that were delightful to behold. In the center of the main hall a large fountain played its columns of spray up to the glass-domed roof, through which the sun shone down on the water and upon the lovely plants that grew in the big basin.

Now that she knew where he lived, many an evening and many a night she spent there in the sea. She swam much closer to shore than any of her sisters would dare venture, and she even went far up a narrow stream, under the splendid marble balcony that cast its long shadow in the water. Here she used to sit and watch the young Prince when he thought himself quite alone in the bright moonlight.

On many evenings she saw him sail out in his fine boat, with music playing and flags a-flutter. She would peep out through the green rushes, and if the wind blew her long silver veil, anyone who saw it mistook it for a swan spreading its wings.

On many nights she saw the fishermen come out to sea with their torches, and heard them tell about how kind the young Prince was. This made her proud to think that it was she who had saved his life when he was buffeted about, half dead among the waves. And she thought of how softly his head had rested on her breast, and how tenderly she had kissed him, though he knew nothing of all this nor could he even dream of it.

Increasingly she grew to like human beings, and more and more she longed to live among them. Their world seemed so much wider than her own, for they could skim over the sea in ships, and mount up into the lofty peaks high over the clouds, and their lands stretched out in woods and fields farther than the eye could see. There was so much she wanted to know. Her sisters could not answer all her questions, so she asked her old grandmother, who knew about the "upper world," which was what she said was the right name for the countries above the sea.

"If men aren't drowned," the little mermaid asked, "do they live on forever? Don't they die, as we do down here in the sea?"

"Yes," the old lady said, "they too must die, and their lifetimes are even shorter than ours. We can live to be three hundred years old, but when we perish we turn into mere foam on the sea, and haven't even a grave down here among our dear ones. We have no immortal soul, no life hereafter. We are like the green seaweed - once cut down, it never grows again. Human beings, on the contrary, have a soul which lives forever, long after their bodies have turned to clay. It rises through thin air, up to the shining stars. Just as we rise through the water to see the lands on earth, so men rise up to beautiful places unknown, which we shall never see."

"Why weren't we given an immortal soul?" the little mermaid sadly asked. "I would gladly give up my three hundred years if I could be a human being only for a day, and later share in that heavenly realm."

"You must not think about that," said the old lady. "We fare much more happily and are much better off than the folk up there."

"Then I must also die and float as foam upon the sea, not hearing the music of the waves, and seeing neither the beautiful flowers nor the red sun! Can't I do anything at all to win an immortal soul?"

"No," her grandmother answered, "not unless a human being loved you so much that you meant more to him than his father and mother. If his every thought and his whole heart cleaved to you so that he would let a priest join his right hand to yours and would promise to be faithful here and throughout all eternity, then his soul would dwell in your body, and you would share in the happiness of mankind. He would give you a soul and yet keep his own. But that can never come to pass. The very thing that is your greatest beauty here in the sea - your fish tail - would be considered ugly on land. They have such poor taste that to be thought beautiful there you have to have two awkward props which they call legs."

The little mermaid sighed and looked unhappily at her fish tail.

"Come, let us be gay!" the old lady said. "Let us leap and bound throughout the three hundred years that we have to live. Surely that is time and to spare, and afterwards we shall be glad enough to rest in our graves. - We are holding a court ball this evening."

This was a much more glorious affair than is ever to be seen on earth. The walls and the ceiling of the great ballroom were made of massive but transparent glass. Many hundreds of huge rose-red and grass-green shells stood on each side in rows, with the blue flames that burned in each shell illuminating the whole room and shining through the walls so clearly that it was quite bright in the sea outside. You could see the countless fish, great and small, swimming toward the glass walls. On some of them the scales gleamed purplish-red, while others were silver and gold. Across the floor of the hall ran a wide stream of water, and upon this the mermaids and mermen danced to their own entrancing songs. Such beautiful voices are not to be heard among the people who live on land. The little mermaid sang more sweetly than anyone else, and everyone applauded her. For a moment her heart was happy, because she knew she had the loveliest voice of all, in the sea or on the land. But her thoughts soon strayed to the world up above. She could not forget the charming Prince, nor her sorrow that she did not have an immortal soul like his. Therefore she stole out of her father's palace and, while everything there was song and gladness, she sat sadly in her own little garden.

Then she heard a bugle call through the water, and she thought, "That must mean he is sailing up there, he whom I love more than my father or mother, he of whom I am always thinking, and in whose hands I would so willingly trust my lifelong happiness. I dare do anything to win him and to gain an immortal soul. While my sisters are dancing here, in my father's palace, I shall visit the sea witch of whom I have always been so afraid. Perhaps she will be able to advise me and help me."

The little mermaid set out from her garden toward the whirlpools that raged in front of the witch's dwelling. She had never gone that way before. No flowers grew there, nor any seaweed. Bare and gray, the sands extended to the whirlpools, where like roaring mill wheels the waters whirled and snatched everything within their reach down to the bottom of the sea. Between these tumultuous whirlpools she had to thread her way to reach the witch's waters, and then for a long stretch the only trail lay through a hot seething mire, which the witch called her peat marsh. Beyond it her house lay in the middle of a weird forest, where all the trees and shrubs were polyps, half animal and half plant. They looked like hundred-headed snakes growing out of the soil. All their branches were long, slimy arms, with fingers like wriggling worms. They squirmed, joint by joint, from their roots to their outermost tentacles, and whatever they could lay hold of they twined around and never let go. The little mermaid was terrified, and stopped at the edge of the forest. Her heart thumped with fear and she nearly turned back, but then she remembered the Prince and the souls that men have, and she summoned her courage. She bound her long flowing locks closely about her head so that the polyps could not catch hold of them, folded her arms across her breast, and darted through the water like a fish, in among the slimy polyps that stretched out their writhing arms and fingers to seize her. She saw that every one of them held something that it had caught with its hundreds of little tentacles, and to which it clung as with strong hoops of steel. The white bones of men who had perished at sea and sunk to these depths could be seen in the polyps' arms. Ships' rudders, and seamen's chests, and the skeletons of land animals had also fallen into their clutches, but the most ghastly sight of all was a little mermaid whom they had caught and strangled.

She reached a large muddy clearing in the forest, where big fat water snakes slithered about, showing their foul yellowish bellies. In the middle of this clearing was a house built of the bones of shipwrecked men, and there sat the sea witch, letting a toad eat out of her mouth just as we might feed sugar to a little canary bird. She called the ugly fat water snakes her little chickabiddies, and let them crawl and sprawl about on her spongy bosom.

"I know exactly what you want," said the sea witch. "It is very foolish of you, but just the same you shall have your way, for it will bring you to grief, my proud princess. You want to get rid of your fish tail and have two props instead, so that you can walk about like a human creature, and have the young Prince fall in love with you, and win him and an immortal soul besides." At this, the witch gave such a loud cackling laugh that the toad and the snakes were shaken to the ground, where they lay writhing.

"You are just in time," said the witch. "After the sun comes up tomorrow, a whole year would have to go by before I could be of any help to you. J shall compound you a draught, and before sunrise you must swim to the shore with it, seat yourself on dry land, and drink the draught down. Then your tail will divide and shrink until it becomes what the people on earth call a pair of shapely legs. But it will hurt; it will feel as if a sharp sword slashed through you. Everyone who sees you will say that you are the most graceful human being they have ever laid eyes on, for you will keep your gliding movement and no dancer will be able to tread as lightly as you. But every step you take will feel as if you were treading upon knife blades so sharp that blood must flow. I am willing to help you, but are you willing to suffer all this?"

"Yes," the little mermaid said in a trembling voice, as she thought of the Prince and of gaining a human soul.

"Remember!" said the witch. "Once you have taken a human form, you can never be a mermaid again. You can never come back through the waters to your sisters, or to your father's palace. And if you do not win the love of the Prince so completely that for your sake he forgets his father and mother, cleaves to you with his every thought and his whole heart, and lets the priest join your hands in marriage, then you will win no immortal soul. If he marries someone else, your heart will break on the very next morning, and you will become foam of the sea."

"I shall take that risk," said the little mermaid, but she turned as pale as death.

"Also, you will have to pay me," said the witch, "and it is no trifling price that I'm asking. You have the sweetest voice of anyone down here at the bottom of the sea, and while I don't doubt that you would like to captivate the Prince with it, you must give this voice to me. I will take the very best thing that you have, in return for my sovereign draught. I must pour my own blood in it to make the drink as sharp as a two-edged sword."

"But if you take my voice," said the little mermaid, "what will be left to me?"

"Your lovely form," the witch told her, "your gliding movements, and your eloquent eyes. With these you can easily enchant a human heart. Well, have you lost your courage? Stick out your little tongue and I shall cut it off. I'll have my price, and you shall have the potent draught."

"Go ahead," said the little mermaid.

The witch hung her caldron over the flames, to brew the draught. "Cleanliness is a good thing," she said, as she tied her snakes in a knot and scoured out the pot with them. Then she pricked herself in the chest and let her black blood splash into the caldron. Steam swirled up from it, in such ghastly shapes that anyone would have been terrified by them. The witch constantly threw new ingredients into the caldron, and it started to boil with a sound like that of a crocodile shedding tears. When the draught was ready at last, it looked as clear as the purest water.

"There's your draught," said the witch. And she cut off the tongue of the little mermaid, who now was dumb and could neither sing nor talk.

"If the polyps should pounce on you when you walk back through my wood," the witch said, "just spill a drop of this brew upon them and their tentacles will break in a thousand pieces." But there was no need of that, for the polyps curled up in terror as soon as they saw the bright draught. It glittered in the little mermaid's hand as if it were a shining star. So she soon traversed the forest, the marsh, and the place of raging whirlpools.

She could see her father's palace. The lights had been snuffed out in the great ballroom, and doubtless everyone in the palace was asleep, but she dared not go near them, now that she was stricken dumb and was leaving her home forever. Her heart felt as if it would break with grief. She tip-toed into the garden, took one flower from each of her sisters' little plots, blew a thousand kisses toward the palace, and then mounted up through the dark blue sea.

The sun had not yet risen when she saw the Prince's palace.

As she climbed his splendid marble staircase, the moon was shining clear. The little mermaid swallowed the bitter, fiery draught, and it was as if a two-edged sword struck through her frail body. She swooned away, and lay there as if she were dead. When the sun rose over the sea she awoke and felt a flash of pain, but directly in front of her stood the handsome young Prince, gazing at her with his coal-black eyes. Lowering her gaze, she saw that her fish tail was gone, and that she had the loveliest pair of white legs any young maid could hope to have. But she was naked, so she clothed herself in her own long hair.

The Prince asked who she was, and how she came to be there. Her deep blue eyes looked at him tenderly but very sadly, for she could not speak. Then he took her hand and led her into his palace. Every footstep felt as if she were walking on the blades and points of sharp knives, just as the witch had foretold, but she gladly endured it. She moved as lightly as a bubble as she walked beside the Prince. He and all who saw her marveled at the grace of her gliding walk.

Once clad in the rich silk and muslin garments that were provided for her, she was the loveliest person in all the palace, though she was dumb and could neither sing nor speak. Beautiful slaves, attired in silk and cloth of gold, came to sing before the Prince and his royal parents. One of them sang more sweetly than all the others, and when the Prince smiled at her and clapped his hands, the little mermaid felt very unhappy, for she knew that she herself used to sing much more sweetly.

"Oh," she thought, "if he only knew that I parted with my voice forever so that I could be near him."

Graceful slaves now began to dance to the most wonderful music. Then the little mermaid lifted her shapely white arms, rose up on the tips of her toes, and skimmed over the floor. No one had ever danced so well. Each movement set off her beauty to better and better advantage, and her eyes spoke more directly to the heart than any of the singing slaves could do.

She charmed everyone, and especially the Prince, who called her his dear little foundling. She danced time and again, though every time she touched the floor she felt as if she were treading on sharp-edged steel. The Prince said he would keep her with him always, and that she was to have a velvet pillow to sleep on outside his door.

He had a page's suit made for her, so that she could go with him on horseback. They would ride through the sweet scented woods, where the green boughs brushed her shoulders, and where the little birds sang among the fluttering leaves.

She climbed up high mountains with the Prince, and though her tender feet bled so that all could see it, she only laughed and followed him on until they could see the clouds driving far below, like a flock of birds in flight to distant lands.

At home in the Prince's palace, while the others slept at night, she would go down the broad marble steps to cool her burning feet in the cold sea water, and then she would recall those who lived beneath the sea. One night her sisters came by, arm in arm, singing sadly as they breasted the waves. When she held out her hands toward them, they knew who she was, and told her how unhappy she had made them all. They came to see her every night after that, and once far, far out to sea, she saw her old grandmother, who had not been up to the surface this many a year. With her was the sea king, with his crown upon his head. They stretched out their hands to her, but they did not venture so near the land as her sisters had.

Day after day she became more dear to the Prince, who loved her as one would love a good little child, but he never thought of making her his Queen. Yet she had to be his wife or she would never have an immortal soul, and on the morning after his wedding she would turn into foam on the waves.

"Don't you love me best of all?" the little mermaid's eyes seemed to question him, when he took her in his arms and kissed her lovely forehead.

"Yes, you are most dear to me," said the Prince, "for you have the kindest heart. You love me more than anyone else does, and you look so much like a young girl I once saw but never shall find again. I was on a ship that was wrecked, and the waves cast me ashore near a holy temple, where many young girls performed the rituals. The youngest of them found me beside the sea and saved my life. Though I saw her no more than twice, she is the only person in all the world whom I could love. But you are so much like her that you almost replace the memory of her in my heart. She belongs to that holy temple, therefore it is my good fortune that I have you. We shall never part."

"Alas, he doesn't know it was I who saved his life," the little mermaid thought. "I carried him over the sea to the garden where the temple stands. I hid behind the foam and watched to see if anyone would come. I saw the pretty maid he loves better than me." A sigh was the only sign of her deep distress, for a mermaid cannot cry. "He says that the other maid belongs to the holy temple. She will never come out into the world, so they will never see each other again. It is I who will care for him, love him, and give all my life to him."

Now rumors arose that the Prince was to wed the beautiful daughter of a neighboring King, and that it was for this reason he was having such a superb ship made ready to sail. The rumor ran that the Prince's real interest in visiting the neighboring kingdom was to see the King's daughter, and that he was to travel with a lordly retinue. The little mermaid shook her head and smiled, for she knew the Prince's thoughts far better than anyone else did.

"I am forced to make this journey," he told her. "I must visit the beautiful Princess, for this is my parents' wish, but they would not have me bring her home as my bride against my own will, and I can never love her. She does not resemble the lovely maiden in the temple, as you do, and if I were to choose a bride, I would sooner choose you, my dear mute foundling with those telling eyes of yours." And he kissed her on the mouth, fingered her long hair, and laid his head against her heart so that she came to dream of mortal happiness and an immortal soul.

"I trust you aren't afraid of the sea, my silent child ' he said, as they went on board the magnificent vessel that was to carry them to the land of the neighboring King. And he told her stories of storms, of ships becalmed, of strange deep-sea fish, and of the wonders that divers have seen. She smiled at such stories, for no one knew about the bottom of the sea as well as she did.

In the clear moonlight, when everyone except the man at the helm was asleep, she sat on the side of the ship gazing down through the transparent water, and fancied she could catch glimpses of her father's palace. On the topmost tower stood her old grandmother, wearing her silver crown and looking up at the keel of the ship through the rushing waves. Then her sisters rose to the surface, looked at her sadly, and wrung their white hands. She smiled and waved, trying to let them know that all went well and that she was happy. But along came the cabin boy, and her sisters dived out of sight so quickly that the boy supposed the flash of white he had seen was merely foam on the sea.

Next morning the ship came in to the harbor of the neighboring King's glorious city. All the church bells chimed, and trumpets were sounded from all the high towers, while the soldiers lined up with flying banners and glittering bayonets. Every day had a new festivity, as one ball or levee followed another, but the Princess was still to appear. They said she was being brought up in some far-away sacred temple, where she was learning every royal virtue. But she came at last.

The little mermaid was curious to see how beautiful this

Princess was, and she had to grant that a more exquisite figure she had never seen. The Princess's skin was clear and fair, and behind the long, dark lashes her deep blue eyes were smiling and devoted.

"It was you!" the Prince cried. "You are the one who saved me when I lay like a dead man beside the sea." He clasped the blushing bride of his choice in his arms. "Oh, I am happier than a man should be!" he told his little mermaid. "My fondest dream - that which I never dared to hope - has come true. You will share in my great joy, for you love me more than anyone does."

The little mermaid kissed his hand and felt that her heart was beginning to break. For the morning after his wedding day would see her dead and turned to watery foam.

All the church bells rang out, and heralds rode through the streets to announce the wedding. Upon every altar sweet-scented oils were burned in costly silver lamps. The priests swung their censers, the bride and the bridegroom joined their hands, and the bishop blessed their marriage. The little mermaid, clothed in silk and cloth of gold, held the bride's train, but she was deaf to the wedding march and blind to the holy ritual. Her thought turned on her last night upon earth, and on all she had lost in this world.

That same evening, the bride and bridegroom went aboard the ship. Cannon thundered and banners waved. On the deck of the ship a royal pavilion of purple and gold was set up, and furnished with luxurious cushions. Here the wedded couple were to sleep on that calm, clear night. The sails swelled in the breeze, and the ship glided so lightly that it scarcely seemed to move over the quiet sea. All nightfall brightly colored lanterns were lighted, and the mariners merrily danced on the deck. The little mermaid could not forget that first time she rose from the depths of the sea and looked on at such pomp and happiness. Light as a swallow pursued by his enemies, she joined in the

whirling dance. Everyone cheered her, for never had she
danced so wonderfully. Her tender feet felt as if they were
pierced by daggers, but she did not feel it. Her heart suffered
far greater pain. She knew that this was the last evening that
she ever would see him for whom she had forsaken her home
and family, for whom she had sacrificed her lovely voice and
suffered such constant torment, while he knew nothing of
all these things. It was the last night that she would breathe
the same air with him, or look upon deep waters or the star
fields of the blue sky. A never-ending night, without thought
and without dreams, awaited her who had no soul and could
not get one. The merrymaking lasted long after midnight, yet
she laughed and danced on despite the thought of death she
carried in her heart. The Prince kissed his beautiful bride and
she toyed with his coal-black hair. Hand in hand, they went to
rest in the magnificent pavilion.

A hush came over the ship. Only the helmsman remained
on deck as the little mermaid leaned her white arms on the
bulwarks and looked to the east to see the first red hint of
daybreak, for she knew that the first flash of the sun would
strike her dead. Then she saw her sisters rise up among the
waves. They were as pale as she, and there was no sign of their
lovely long hair that the breezes used to blow. It had all been
cut off.

'We have given our hair to the witch," they said, "so that
she would send you help, and save you from death tonight.
She gave us a knife. Here it is. See the sharp blade! Before the
sun rises, you must strike it into the Prince's heart, and when
his warm blood bathes your feet they will grow together and
become a fish tail. Then you will be a mermaid again, able to
come back to us in the sea, and live out your three hundred
years before you die and turn into dead salt sea foam. Make
haste! He or you must die before sunrise. Our old grandmother
is so grief-stricken that her white hair is falling fast, just as ours
did under the witch's scissors. Kill the Prince and come back

          Goldilocks and the Three Bears and other writings

to us. Hurry! Hurry! See that red glow in the heavens! In a few minutes the sun will rise and you must die." So saying, they gave a strange deep sigh and sank beneath the waves.

The little mermaid parted the purple curtains of the tent and saw the beautiful bride asleep with her head on the Prince's breast. The mermaid bent down and kissed his shapely forehead. She looked at the sky, fast reddening for the break of day. She looked at the sharp knife and again turned her eyes toward the Prince, who in his sleep murmured the name of his bride. His thoughts were all for her, and the knife blade trembled in the mermaid's hand. But then she flung it from her, far out over the waves. Where it fell the waves were red, as if bubbles of blood seethed in the water. With eyes already glazing she looked once more at the Prince, hurled herself over the bulwarks into the sea, and felt her body dissolve in foam.

The sun rose up from the waters. Its beams fell, warm and kindly, upon the chill sea foam, and the little mermaid did not feel the hand of death. In the bright sunlight overhead, she saw hundreds of fair ethereal beings. They were so transparent that through them she could see the ship's white sails and the red clouds in the sky. Their voices were sheer music, but so spirit-like that no human ear could detect the sound, just as no eye on earth could see their forms. Without wings, they floated as light as the air itself. The little mermaid discovered that she was shaped like them, and that she was gradually rising up out of the foam.

'Who are you, toward whom I rise?" she asked, and her voice sounded like those above her, so spiritual that no music on earth could match it.

"We are the daughters of the air," they answered. "A mermaid has no immortal soul, and can never get one unless she wins the love of a human being. Her eternal life must depend upon a power outside herself. The daughters of the air do not have an immortal soul either, but they can earn one by their good deeds. We fly to the south, where the hot poisonous air kills human beings unless we bring cool breezes. We carry the scent of flowers through the air, bringing freshness and healing balm wherever we go. When for three hundred years we have tried to do all the good that we can, we are given an immortal soul and a share in mankind's eternal bliss. You, poor little mermaid, have tried with your whole heart to do this too. Your suffering and your loyalty have raised you up into the realm of airy spirits, and now in the course of three hundred years you may earn by your good deeds a soul that will never die."

The little mermaid lifted her clear bright eyes toward God's sun, and for the first time her eyes were wet with tears.

On board the ship all was astir and lively again. She saw the Prince and his fair bride in search of her. Then they gazed sadly into the seething foam, as if they knew she had hurled herself into the waves. Unseen by them, she kissed the bride's forehead, smiled upon the Prince, and rose up with the other daughters of the air to the rose-red clouds that sailed on high.

"This is the way that we shall rise to the kingdom of God, after three hundred years have passed."

"We may get there even sooner," one spirit whispered. "Unseen, we fly into the homes of men, where there are children, and for every day on which we find a good child who pleases his parents and deserves their love, God shortens our days of trial. The child does not know when we float through his room, but when we smile at him in approval one year is taken from our three hundred. But if we see a naughty, mischievous child we must shed tears of sorrow, and each tear adds a day to the time of our trial."

     Goldilocks and the Three Bears and other writings

The Three Billy-Goats Gruff

by Peter Christen Asbjørnsen, Jørgen Moe

Once upon a time there were three billy goats, who were to go up to the hillside to make themselves fat, and the name of all three was "Gruff."

On the way up was a bridge over a cascading stream they had to cross; and under the bridge lived a great ugly troll , with eyes as big as saucers, and a nose as long as a poker.

So first of all came the youngest Billy Goat Gruff to cross the bridge.

"Trip, trap, trip, trap! " went the bridge.

"Who's that tripping over my bridge?" roared the troll.

"Oh, it is only I, the tiniest Billy Goat Gruff , and I'm going up to the hillside to make myself fat," said the billy goat, with such a small voice.

"Now, I'm coming to gobble you up," said the troll.

"Oh, no! pray don't take me. I'm too little, that I am," said the billy goat. "Wait a bit till the second Billy Goat Gruff comes. He's much bigger."

"Well, be off with you," said the troll.

A little while after came the second Billy Goat Gruff to cross the bridge.

Trip, trap, trip, trap, trip, trap, went the bridge.

"Who's that tripping over my bridge?" roared the troll.

"Oh, it's the second Billy Goat Gruff , and I'm going up to the hillside to make myself fat," said the billy goat, who hadn't such a small voice.

"Now I'm coming to gobble you up," said the troll.

"Oh, no! Don't take me. Wait a little till the big Billy Goat Gruff comes. He's much bigger."

"Very well! Be off with you," said the troll.

But just then up came the big Billy Goat Gruff .

Trip, trap, trip, trap, trip, trap! went the bridge, for the billy goat was so heavy that the bridge creaked and groaned under him.

"Who's that tramping over my bridge?" roared the troll.

"It's I! The big Billy Goat Gruff ," said the billy goat, who had an ugly hoarse voice of his own.

"Now I 'm coming to gobble you up," roared the troll.

Well, come along! I've got two spears,

And I'll poke your eyeballs out at your ears;

I've got besides two curling-stones,

And I'll crush you to bits, body and bones.

That was what the big billy goat said. And then he flew at the troll, and poked his eyes out with his horns, and crushed him to bits, body and bones, and tossed him out into the cascade, and after that he went up to the hillside. There the billy goats got so fat they were scarcely able to walk home again. And if the fat hasn't fallen off them, why, they're still fat; and so,

Snip, snap, snout.

This tale's told out.

      Goldilocks and the Three Bears and other writings

How the Moon Became Beautiful

by Anonymous

The Moon is very beautiful with his round, bright face which shines with soft and gentle light on all the world of man. But once there was a time when he was not so beautiful as he is now. Six thousand years ago the face of the Moon became changed in a single night. Before that time his face had been so dark and gloomy that no one liked to look at him, and for this reason he was always very sad.

One day he complained to the flowers and to the stars— for they were the only things that would ever look in his face.

He said, "I do not like to be the Moon. I wish I were a star or a flower. If I were a star, even the smallest one, some great general would care for me; but alas! I am only the Moon and no one likes me. If I could only be a flower and grow in a garden where the beautiful earth women come, they would place me in their hair and praise my fragrance and beauty. Or, if I could even grow in the wilderness where no one could see, the birds would surely come and sing sweet songs for me. But I am only the Moon and no one honors me."

The stars answered and said, "We can not help you. We were born here and we can not leave our places. We never had any one to help us. We do our duty, we work all the day and twinkle in the dark night to make the skies more beautiful.— But that is all we can do," they added, as they smiled coldly at the sorrowful Moon.

Then the flowers smiled sweetly and said, "We do not know how we can help you. We live always in one place—in a garden near the most beautiful maiden in all the world. As she is kind

to every one in trouble we will tell her about you. We love her
very much and she loves us. Her name is Tseh-N'io." Still the
Moon was sad. So one evening he went to see the beautiful
maiden Tseh-N'io. And when he saw her he loved her at once.
He said, "Your face is very beautiful. I wish that you would
come to me, and that my face would be as your face. Your
motions are gentle and full of grace. Come with me and we
will be as one—and perfect. I know that even the worst people
in all the world would have only to look at you and they would
love you. Tell me, how did you come to be so beautiful?"

"I have always lived with those who were gentle and
happy, and I believe that is the cause of beauty and goodness,"
answered Tseh-N'io.

And so the Moon went every night to see the maiden. He
knocked on her window, and she came. And when he saw how
gentle and beautiful she was, his love grew stronger, and he
wished more and more to be with her always.

One day Tseh-N'io said to her mother, "I should like to
go to the Moon and live always with him. Will you allow me
to go?"

Her mother thought so little of the question that she made
no reply, and Tseh-N'io told her friends that she was going to
be the Moon's bride.

In a few days she was gone. Her mother searched
everywhere but could not find her. And one of Tseh-N'io's
friends said,—"She has gone with the Moon, for he asked her
many times."

A year and a year passed by and Tseh-N'io, the gentle and
beautiful earth maiden, did not return. Then the people said,
"She has gone forever. She is with the Moon."

The face of the Moon is very beautiful now. It is happy and
bright and gives a soft, gentle light to all the world. And there

are those who say that the Moon is now like Tseh-N'io, who
was once the most beautiful of all earth maidens.

The Last Dream of Old Oak

by Hans Christian Andersen

IN the forest, high up on the steep shore, and not far from the open seacoast, stood a very old oak-tree. It was just three hundred and sixty-five years old, but that long time was to the tree as the same number of days might be to us; we wake by day and sleep by night, and then we have our dreams. It is different with the tree; it is obliged to keep awake through three seasons of the year, and does not get any sleep till winter comes. Winter is its time for rest; its night after the long day of spring, summer, and autumn. On many a warm summer, the Ephemera, the flies that exist for only a day, had fluttered about the old oak, enjoyed life and felt happy and if, for a moment, one of the tiny creatures rested on one of his large fresh leaves, the tree would always say, "Poor little creature! your whole life consists only of a single day. How very short. It must be quite melancholy."

"Melancholy! what do you mean?" the little creature would always reply. "Everything around me is so wonderfully bright and warm, and beautiful, that it makes me joyous."

"But only for one day, and then it is all over."

"Over!" repeated the fly; "what is the meaning of all over? Are you all over too?"

"No; I shall very likely live for thousands of your days, and my day is whole seasons long; indeed it is so long that you could never reckon it out."

"No? then I don't understand you. You may have thousands of my days, but I have thousands of moments in which I can be merry and happy. Does all the beauty of the world cease when you die?"

"No," replied the tree; "it will certainly last much longer,—infinitely longer than I can even think of." "Well, then," said the little fly, "we have the same time to live; only we reckon differently." And the little creature danced and floated in the air, rejoicing in her delicate wings of gauze and velvet, rejoicing in the balmy breezes, laden with the fragrance of clover-fields and wild roses, elder-blossoms and honeysuckle, from the garden hedges, wild thyme, primroses, and mint, and the scent of all these was so strong that the perfume almost intoxicated the little fly. The long and beautiful day had been so full of joy and sweet delights, that when the sun sank low it felt tired of all its happiness and enjoyment. Its wings could sustain it no longer, and gently and slowly it glided down upon the soft waving blades of grass, nodded its little head as well as it could nod, and slept peacefully and sweetly. The fly was dead.

"Poor little Ephemera!" said the oak; "what a terribly short life!" And so, on every summer day the dance was repeated, the same questions asked, and the same answers given. The same thing was continued through many generations of Ephemera; all of them felt equally merry and equally happy.

The oak remained awake through the morning of spring, the noon of summer, and the evening of autumn; its time of rest, its night drew nigh—winter was coming. Already the storms were singing, "Good-night, good-night." Here fell a leaf and there fell a leaf. "We will rock you and lull you. Go to sleep, go to sleep. We will sing you to sleep, and shake you to sleep, and it will do your old twigs good; they will even crackle with pleasure. Sleep sweetly, sleep sweetly, it is your three-hundred-and-sixty-fifth night. Correctly speaking, you are but a youngster in the world. Sleep sweetly, the clouds will drop snow upon you, which will be quite a cover-lid, warm and sheltering to your feet. Sweet sleep to you, and pleasant dreams." And there stood the oak, stripped of all its leaves, left to rest during the whole of a long winter, and to dream many dreams of events that had happened in its life, as in the dreams of men. The great tree had once been small; indeed, in its cradle it had been an acorn. According to human computation, it was now in the fourth century of its existence. It was the largest and best tree in the forest. Its summit towered above all the other trees, and could be seen far out at sea, so that it served as a landmark to the sailors. It had no idea how many eyes looked eagerly for it. In its topmost branches the wood-pigeon built her nest, and the cuckoo carried out his usual vocal performances, and his well-known notes echoed amid the boughs; and in autumn, when the leaves looked like beaten copper plates, the birds of passage would come and rest upon the branches before taking their flight across the sea. But now it was winter, the tree stood leafless, so that every one could see how crooked and bent were the branches that sprang forth from the trunk. Crows and rooks came by turns and sat on them, and talked of the hard times which were beginning, and how difficult it was in winter to obtain food.

It was just about holy Christmas time that the tree dreamed a dream. The tree had, doubtless, a kind of feeling that the festive time had arrived, and in his dream fancied he heard the bells ringing from all the churches round, and yet it seemed to him to be a beautiful summer's day, mild and warm. His mighty summits was crowned with spreading fresh green foliage; the sunbeams played among the leaves and branches, and the air was full of fragrance from herb and blossom; painted butterflies chased each other; the summer flies danced around him, as if the world had been created merely for them to dance and be merry in. All that had happened to the tree during every year of his life seemed to pass before him, as in a festive procession. He saw the knights of olden times and noble ladies ride by through the wood on their gallant steeds, with plumes waving in their hats, and falcons on their wrists. The hunting horn sounded, and the dogs barked. He

   Goldilocks and the Three Bears and other writings

saw hostile warriors, in colored dresses and glittering armor, with spear and halberd, pitching their tents, and anon striking them. The watchfires again blazed, and men sang and slept under the hospitable shelter of the tree. He saw lovers meet in quiet happiness near him in the moonshine, and carve the initials of their names in the grayish-green bark on his trunk. Once, but long years had intervened since then, guitars and Eolian harps had been hung on his boughs by merry travellers; now they seemed to hang there again, and he could hear their marvellous tones. The wood-pigeons cooed as if to explain the feelings of the tree, and the cuckoo called out to tell him how many summer days he had yet to live. Then it seemed as if new life was thrilling through every fibre of root and stem and leaf, rising even to the highest branches. The tree felt itself stretching and spreading out, while through the root beneath the earth ran the warm vigor of life. As he grew higher and still higher, with increased strength, his topmost boughs became broader and fuller; and in proportion to his growth, so was his self-satisfaction increased, and with it arose a joyous longing to grow higher and higher, to reach even to the warm, bright sun itself. Already had his topmost branches pierced the clouds, which floated beneath them like troops of birds of passage, or large white swans; every leaf seemed gifted with sight, as if it possessed eyes to see. The stars became visible in broad daylight, large and sparkling, like clear and gentle eyes. They recalled to the memory the well-known look in the eyes of a child, or in the eyes of lovers who had once met beneath the branches of the old oak. These were wonderful and happy moments for the old tree, full of peace and joy; and yet, amidst all this happiness, the tree felt a yearning, longing desire that all the other trees, bushes, herbs, and flowers beneath him, might be able also to rise higher, as he had done, and to see all this splendor, and experience the same happiness. The grand, majestic oak could not be quite happy in the midst of his enjoyment, while all the rest, both great and small, were not with him. And this feeling of yearning trembled through every branch, through every leaf, as warmly and fervently as if they had been the fibres of a human heart. The summit of the tree waved to and fro, and bent downwards as if in his silent longing he sought for something. Then there came to him the fragrance of thyme, followed by the more powerful scent of honeysuckle and violets; and he fancied he heard the note of the cuckoo. At length his longing was satisfied. Up through the clouds came the green summits of the forest trees, and beneath him, the oak saw them rising, and growing higher and higher. Bush and herb shot upward, and some even tore themselves up by the roots to rise more quickly. The birch-tree was the quickest of all. Like a lightning flash the slender stem shot upwards in a zigzag line, the branches spreading around it like green gauze and banners. Every native of the wood, even to the brown and feathery rushes, grew with the rest, while the birds ascended with the melody of song. On a blade of grass, that fluttered in the air like a long, green ribbon, sat a grasshopper, cleaning his wings with his legs. May beetles hummed, the bees murmured, the birds sang, each in his own way; the air was filled with the sounds of song and gladness.

"But where is the little blue flower that grows by the water?" asked the oak, "and the purple bell-flower, and the daisy?" You see the oak wanted to have them all with him.

"Here we are, we are here," sounded in voice and song.

"But the beautiful thyme of last summer, where is that? and the lilies-of-the-valley, which last year covered the earth with their bloom? and the wild apple-tree with its lovely blossoms, and all the glory of the wood, which has flourished year after year? even what may have but now sprouted forth could be with us here."

"We are here, we are here," sounded voices higher in the air, as if they had flown there beforehand.

"Why this is beautiful, too beautiful to be believed," said

the oak in a joyful tone. "I have them all here, both great and small; not one has been forgotten. Can such happiness be imagined?" It seemed almost impossible.

"In heaven with the Eternal God, it can be imagined, and it is possible," sounded the reply through the air.

And the old tree, as it still grew upwards and onwards, felt that his roots were loosening themselves from the earth.

"It is right so, it is best," said the tree, "no fetters hold me now. I can fly up to the very highest point in light and glory. And all I love are with me, both small and great. All—all are here."

Such was the dream of the old oak: and while he dreamed, a mighty storm came rushing over land and sea, at the holy Christmas time. The sea rolled in great billows towards the shore. There was a cracking and crushing heard in the tree. The root was torn from the ground just at the moment when in his dream he fancied it was being loosened from the earth. He fell—his three hundred and sixty-five years were passed as the single day of the Ephemera. On the morning of Christmas-day, when the sun rose, the storm had ceased. From all the churches sounded the festive bells, and from every hearth, even of the smallest hut, rose the smoke into the blue sky, like the smoke from the festive thank-offerings on the Druids' altars. The sea gradually became calm, and on board a great ship that had withstood the tempest during the night, all the flags were displayed, as a token of joy and festivity. "The tree is down! The old oak,—our landmark on the coast!" exclaimed the sailors. "It must have fallen in the storm of last night. Who can replace it? Alas! no one." This was a funeral oration over the old tree; short, but well-meant. There it lay stretched on the snow-covered shore, and over it sounded the notes of a song from the ship—a song of Christmas joy, and of the redemption of the soul of man, and of eternal life through Christ's atoning blood.

"Sing aloud on the happy morn,

All is fulfilled, for Christ is born;

With songs of joy let us loudly sing,

'Hallelujahs to Christ our King.'"

Thus sounded the old Christmas carol, and every one on board the ship felt his thoughts elevated, through the song and the prayer, even as the old tree had felt lifted up in its last, its beautiful dream on that Christmas morn.

www.ingramcontent.com/pod-product-compliance
Lightning Source LLC
LaVergne TN
LVHW090020180726
843489LV00008B/2890